A NOTE TO PARENTS

Congratulations on choosing the best in educational materials for your child. By selecting top-quality McGraw-Hill products, you can be assured that the concepts used in our books will reinforce and enhance the skills that are being taught in classrooms nationwide.

And what better way to get young readers excited than with Mercer Mayer's Little Critter, a character loved by children everywhere? Our First Readers offer simple and engaging stories about Little Critter that children can read on their own. Each level incorporates reading skills, colorful illustrations, and challenging activities.

Level 1 – The stories are simple and use repetitive language. Illustrations are highly supportive.
Level 2 - The stories begin to grow in complexity. Language is still repetitive, but it is mixed with more challenging vocabulary.
Level 3 - The stories are more complex. Sentences are longer and more varied.

To help your child make the most of this book, look at the first few pictures in the story and discuss what is happening. Ask your child to predict where the story is going. Then, once your child has read the story, have him or her review the word list and do the activities. This will reinforce vocabulary words from the story and build reading comprehension.

You are your child's first and most influential teacher. No one knows your child the way you do. Tailor your time together to reinforce a newly acquired skill or to overcome a temporary stumbling block. Praise your child's progress and ideas, take delight in his or her imagination, and most of all, enjoy your time together!

Library of Congress Cataloging-in-Publication Data

Mayer, Mercer, 1943-
A day at camp / by Mercer Mayer.
                   p. cm. – (First reader, skills and practice)
"Level 2, Grades PreK-1."
Summary: Despite some misadventures, Little Critter is anxious to go back to day camp.
ISBN 1-57768-634-9 (HC), 1-57768-836-8 (PB)
[1. Day camps—Fiction. 2. Camps—Fiction.] I. Title. II. Series.
PZ7.M462 Day 2003
[E]--dc21
        2002008751

 Children's Publishing

Text Copyright © 2003 McGraw-Hill Children's Publishing.
Art Copyright © 2003 Mercer Mayer.

Send all inquiries to:
McGraw-Hill Children's Publishing
8787 Orion Place
Columbus, OH 43240-4027

Printed in the United States of America.

1-57768-634-9

 A Big Tuna Trading Company, LLC/J. R. Sansevere Book

1 2 3 4 5 6 7 8 9 10 PHXBK 08 07 06 05 04 03

FIRST READERS

Level 2   Grades K–1

A DAY AT CAMP

by Mercer Mayer

 Children's Publishing

Columbus, Ohio

This morning I went to camp.
The bus came to pick me up.
I waved good-bye to Mom.

5

First, we learned how to tie knots.
I tried really hard,
but the rope was too long.
I'll use a shorter rope next time.

Then we hiked down the trail,
but we got lost.
I'll follow the signs next time.

At lunchtime, we had a picnic,
but my lunch bag was empty!

Gator shared his lunch with me.
I'll bring my lunch box next time.

In the afternoon, we went fishing.
I caught a fish that was this big,
but it got away.
I'll use a net next time.

13

After that, we had arts and crafts time.
I made a vase for my mom,
but I used a little too much clay.
I'll make her a cup next time.

15

16

At four o'clock, it was time to go home.
Mom met me at the bus stop.
She loved her vase.
I told her I couldn't wait
to go back to camp next time!

Word List

Read each word in the lists below. Then, find it in the story. Now, make up a new sentence using the word. Say your sentence out loud.

<table>
<tr><td>

Words I Know
camp
bus
time
lunch
fish
vase

</td><td>

Challenge Words
waved
knots
tried
trail
signs
empty
caught

</td></tr>
</table>

Short U Words

Use a separate sheet of paper for these activities.

Change one letter of the word bus to make a new word that goes with the picture.

bus

Change one letter of the word but to make a new word that goes with the picture.

but

Change one letter of the word pup to make a new word that goes with the picture.

pup

Synonyms

Words that have almost the same meaning are called synonyms.

Example: Maurice is happy to have a sandwich.
Molly is glad to have a sandwich.

Point to each word in the left column. Then point to its matching synonym in the right column.

noisy   mom

mother   loud

big   silly

funny   large

Antonyms

Some words have opposite meanings. These words are called antonyms.

Example: Little Sister is a girl.
Little Critter is a boy.

Point to each word in the left column. Then point to its matching antonym in the right column.

morning	**full**
long	**night**
empty	**go**
stop	**short**

Understanding the Story

Point to the picture that shows the first thing that Little Critter did at camp.

Point to the picture that shows what Little Critter did after he went hiking.

On another sheet of paper, draw a picture of something else Little Critter did at camp.

ABC Order

On another sheet of paper, write each set of words in abc order. Look at the first letter of each word to help you.

fish

camp

bus

signs

knots

trail

Answer Key

bus ⟶ bun

but ⟶ bug

pup ⟶ cup

Noisy means the same as loud.

Mother means the same as mom.

Big means the same as large.

Funny means the same as silly.

Morning is the opposite of night.

Long is the opposite of short.

Empty is the opposite of full.

Stop is the opposite of go.

The first thing Little Critter did at camp was to tie a knot.

After he went hiking, Little Critter ate lunch.

Other things Little Critter did at camp include hiking, fishing, making a vase, and riding the bus.

bus
camp
fish

knots
signs
trail